Autumn,

Enjoy!
Please look
on your
Christmas tree
for a bulb like
"Bobby"

J. R. R. Brown

BOBBY BRIGHT'S GREATEST CHRISTMAS EVER

BY
John R. Brooks

ILLUSTRATIONS BY
Miracle Studios

Old Farm Press

All inquiries should be addressed to:
Old Farm Press
4125 Old Farm Road
Oklahoma City, OK 73120

Printed and bound in the United States of America

ISBN – 13: 978-0-9788227-0-5 (hardcover)
ISBN – 10: 0-9788227-0-6 (hardcover)

In Memory Of

My mother Berneice Brooks and grandmother Edna Cowsert for making possible the wonderful memories I have of beautiful Christmas trees, lights, and ornaments, which always made Christmas the most special time of the year.

Special Thanks To

My wife Lisa, who spent countless hours fine tuning and editing the book, and 10-year old son Remington who spent all those early mornings listening to the words written the night before as the first manuscript evolved during the summer of 2004 while we toured and resided in those lovely Paradores in Spain.

Tom Hignite, president of Miracle Studios, and his world class animated illustrators whose dedication to detail and the whole project was outstanding. I salute them by name and the movie and video credentials they have collected and earned through their myriad talents:

   Dan Daly------------The Lion King, Mulan, Lilo & Stitch, Brother
                       Bear, Pocahontas, John Henry.

   Troy Gustafson-----Mulan, John Henry, Lilo & Stitch, Brother Bear,
                       The Hunchback of Notre Dame.

   Greg Peters---------Scooby Doo, Cool World, Once Upon A Forest,
                       Timon & Pumba

   Tim O'Donnell-------Mickey's Christmas Carol, The Great Mouse
                       Detective, Beauty and the Beast, Oliver & Co.

   Mike Lowery--------Tom & Jerry, Animaniacs, Tinytoons,
                       Teenage Mutant Ninja Turtles.

Also to JMP Services of Jackson, WI whose guidance in all matters of editing, design, layout, and the other challenges of putting a book into final form was immeasurable in terms of making this endeavor possible.

Our Family Picture

Contents

Prologue 1

Part One 7

  1 Out of the Closet 8

  2 Testing the Bulbs 13

  3 Danger for Bobby and His Family ... 19

  4 Bobby Takes a Chance 28

  5 Bobby Works His Magic 35

  6 Bobby Puts His Plan to Work 41

  7 Look What Bobby Did 48

  8 Bobby's Plan Saves the Family 53

Part Two 59

  9 Two Weeks Before Christmas 61

 10 Let the Party Begin 69

 11 It's Party Time 71

 12 Night Time December 23rd 74

 13 Christmas Eve Afternoon 81

 14 Remington Meets New Friends 91

 15 Remington Talks. Bobby Listens. .. 96

 16 Bobby Reminisces 98

 17 Late Christmas Night 104

 18 Bobby and Remington Get Closer ... 108

 19 December 28th 115

 20 Good-bye Remington 121

Epilogue 126

Prologue

Just over ten years ago at the largest factory in the world that makes Christmas tree light bulbs, something very strange happened late one hot July afternoon when the air conditioning system failed.

The man in charge of the long, long, long conveyor belt, which sent the newly made bulbs to the machine that placed the bulbs on cords, got very tired and fell asleep because it was so hot.

As he dreamed of the big lunch he had eaten only minutes earlier, his head bobbed back and forth and he snored loudly even though he was only asleep for a few seconds. Just before he was about to awake his head fell forward and he hit his nose on the belt.

"Ouch!" he screamed as he awakened to the burn of the belt on the tip of his nose. Stepping back from the moving belt he gently touched his nose. It hurt, but nothing else seemed wrong and he thought all was okay. However, he was badly wrong.

Looking up he was shocked to see bulbs flying everywhere. Over his head, onto the floor, off the front of his shirt and even on his face where one beautiful new blue bulb smashed into his nose and actually stuck in his nostril.

Now *this* did hurt. The scrape on the end of his nose began to bleed slightly. As bad as it was, it would have been very, very funny if there hadn't been a much bigger problem than a bulb in his nose.

He stepped over as many bulbs as he could among the dozens now rolling around the floor. Reaching for the lever to stop the conveyor belt he gave it a pull. A big bolt of electricity shot from the generator box shocking him for just a couple of seconds.

He jumped backwards and slipped on the rolling bulbs and grabbed for the conveyor belt to keep from falling. When he touched it, the belt SCREECHED to an abrupt stop. The rest of the bulbs on the belt flew off, scattering across the floor, flying off the walls, and landing on other pieces of machinery throughout the giant factory's main floor.

As for him, well, he went KERPLUNK, and hit the floor with a THUMP. Then he heard lots of other workers yelling from all over the factory.

"What's going on?"

"Why did the belt stop?"

"Where are the bulbs?"

People came running into the room to see what had happened.

What they saw were smashed and broken bulbs everywhere. There in front of them lay the man in charge of the conveyor belt.

All of the employees were now staring at him and beginning to laugh and point.

The old man didn't understand why. They should be feeling sorry for him, he thought, but they were laughing instead.

"What have you done, and why do you have a bulb stuck in your nose?" someone shouted.

The old man was so embarrassed by what had occurred, he didn't realize the bulb was still hanging from his nose.

He quickly grabbed the deep blue colored bulb and threw it on the floor as hard as he could.

Everyone was laughing until the boss of the factory came charging into the conveyor belt room. The laughter stopped and they all hustled back to their work areas.

The boss looked at the old man and then at the floor covered with broken bulbs. He looked at the conveyor belt which was empty.

Beneath the belt lay about two dozen bulbs that were not broken. Elsewhere things were in shambles. It was a mess.

"Clean this up!" shouted the boss pointing to the man on the floor.

"I'll see you in my office later, and send those bulbs that aren't broken to the strand machine."

The old man nodded as the boss stomped away. He grabbed a broom and began sweeping the broken glass off the belt onto the floor.

Beautiful bulbs that weren't broken smashed into tiny pieces as they fell.

As he looked down at the debris, the old man was taken back. That blue bulb, which he thought was the darkest blue he had ever seen, was the same one which had stuck in his nose. It was lying on the floor.

When he had tossed it away a moment ago it had clanked off the concrete, bounced into the air and somersaulted forward.

The bulb had bounced three or four times, twisted around like a spinning top, and then rolled into a corner.

As he stood there staring at it, the old man thought, "One tough bulb." Maybe that was the reason he did what he did, although no one will probably ever know for sure. He bent down with a smile on his face and picked through the mess. Brushing away sharp shards of glass, he found the blue bulb and placed it in the palm of his left hand and moved it around. He then played with it for a moment and decided he might keep it as a token from what had happened. But then, just as quickly, he changed his mind again. He didn't need any reminders about this catastrophe. He placed the blue bulb and the few others that weren't broken back on the belt, reached up, and pushed the lever back. The belt slowly whined and twisted itself into motion, and the two dozen bulbs that had survived the accident were carried to the next position and joined together in a strand.

And it's here our story begins.

There will probably be only a few people who read this story of Bobby Bright and actually believe a Christmas tree bulb can talk and also understand human language.

Most will think this is not possible, and maybe they are right.

But will we ever be able to know for sure? Haven't you heard of strange things happening in your city?

Is there a special strand of Christmas tree lights in your home?

Why don't you look and see this Christmas when your folks bring out all of those bags and boxes from where they have been stored all year.

Most of you won't think it's possible and that's okay. But before you say nothing like this could happen, remember, maybe you are like me. Maybe you too will find "Bobby Bright".

If you do, make sure you place him at the front of your Christmas tree.   These next few chapters will explain why.

PART ONE

1
Out of the Closet

Mrs. McGillicuddy always did spring cleaning. It made no difference whether something needed cleaning or not. She ALWAYS did spring cleaning.

That's why Bobby knew it was April. Mrs. McGilli-cuddy ALWAYS did her spring cleaning in April. He didn't know what day it was and it didn't really make any difference. The important thing was that once she finished spring cleaning, he could begin to count the days until the beginning of Christmas season which was always the day after Thanksgiving in the McGillicuddy household.

Bobby knew that carefully counting each day af-ter spring cleaning did not mean he would know exactly when the day after Thanksgiving arrived.

He might still be thinking he and his family had a few more days in their year long dungeon, when in fact, they really didn't.

Now THAT was fun. Getting out early. But then occasionally it worked the other way too. He would count and count the days, and about the time he thought it was time to get out, another day would come and then another, and they would still be buried down at the bottom of the box inside the dark closet.

That's when Bobby would start thinking, *"Oh no! Are they sick? Are they gone this year? Are they not going to have a Christmas tree?"*

But about the time he would just know the very worst was going to happen, and he and his special family were going to be thrown away, or not used that year, he would hear the noises he heard only twice a year.

CREEEAK...."*That's the door!*" someone would always whisper. .... PULL ....TUG .....PULL ....TUG ..... WHOOSH.

And then Mr. McGillicuddy would turn on the light bulb and the brightness would shine through the slit in the top of the giant box where only light bulbs and a very few important ornaments lived for nearly eleven months a year.

And at this very moment Bobby heard those familiar noises.

CREAK.....PULL.....TUG.....PULL......TUG......WHOOSH.

And sure enough someone in Bobby's family whispered, *"That's the door."*

Now came the familiar rumble of other small boxes being moved first. That moment Bobby and all of the Bright family and their relatives looked forward to each year suddenly happened.

Mr. McGillicuddy dragged their box outside into the room and Bobby heard the talking for the first time.

"Do you want the rest of the boxes brought into the game room, honey, or do you want to do the lights first?"

Bobby whispered to the rest of his family what was happening. He knew he didn't have to whisper because Mr. McGillicuddy was always too busy making noise while moving the boxes and he didn't hear very well. He also knew they would not be heard down at the very bottom of the box where they lived every year.

Up above Bobby heard, "What did you say, honey?"

Of course Bobby knew that was one of three things that were absolutely certain to happen.

First----Mrs. McGillicuddy ALWAYS did spring cleaning in April.

Second----Mr. McGillicuddy ALWAYS asked Mrs.

McGillicuddy if she wanted to put the lights on the Christmas tree first.

And third----Mr. McGillicuddy would ALWAYS say, "What did you say, Honey?"

"What did he say? Is he going to open the box? What's going on?"

The questions came from all around him as every member of the Bright family became excited.

"Not so loud," Bobby shouted. Then he realized he was shouting too.

He whispered. *"Be quiet up there. I'll let everyone know what's happening."*

"What is it, John?" Mrs. McGillicuddy's voice was in the distance but getting closer. "Did you say something?"

"I said, 'did you say something'?" Mr. McGillicuddy shouted.

"John, I'm right here. Please, don't shout."

Bobby stuck the nose of his bulb up against the cord and started to laugh. It was the same each year, but he always laughed. The others began to laugh with him.

It hadn't always been that way. There had been a time when the other bulbs didn't like the fact that only Bobby understood human language. But eventually they had accepted the fact. Bobby smiled as he thought about it.

He was the "Bright Bright", no doubt about it. Just then, as the box moved again, he bumped into his Uncle Flicker and Aunt Shining. They had been sleeping next to him all year.

You never knew who you would sleep next to when Christmas was over and you went back in the dungeon. Just depended on how Mr. McGillicuddy wound up the light strands.

Sometimes you were with your mom and dad, and that was always nice. Then there were times the whole family would get twisted up differently and you'd only be able to talk to them, but never see them until Christmas season arrived.

Which of course was always the day after Thanksgiving when Mr. McGillicuddy would drag out the box and ask Mrs. McGillicuddy if she wanted to put the lights on first, and Mrs. McGillicuddy would shout something from the other end of the house and Mr. McGillicuddy would ALWAYS say, "What did you say, honey?"

2

Testing the Bulbs

It happened only three times a year. Suddenly the box was in the air and Mr. McGillicuddy was walking with it to the very large game room that the McGillicuddys laughingly called the "Sports Arena". In the far corner stood this year's Christmas tree in the very same place where it always stood.

"What a feeling," thought Bobby, as he and the other members of this very special family whispered and wondered how long it would be before the other strands were removed, and they could see the light of day, the ceiling of the room, and eventually the big Christmas tree. It would be the first time in 47 weeks.

And it was ALWAYS 47 weeks of waiting, give or take a day or two, because Mr. and Mrs. McGillicuddy ALWAYS put the tree up the day after Thanksgiving and they ALWAYS took the tree down the day after

Christmas.

The box came downward from the arms of Mr. McGillicuddy and inside Bobby felt the other strands shift slightly along with his own family. He heard the top of the box open and he heard the voice of Mr. McGillicuddy.

"Jane, did you say something?"

Bobby heard Mrs. McGillicuddy's high pitched and sometimes irritating voice from the kitchen, which was adjacent to the large game room.

The other strands couldn't understand or hear anything. They were like all the other bulbs in the world. Only the Bright family strand was different.

Only Bobby's family could talk among themselves, except for the two replacement bulbs. Bobby was the only one who understood human language.

Nevertheless, members of his family often joked about how Mrs. McGillicuddy sounded even though they couldn't understand one single word she said.

"What did she say, Bobby?"

"I don't know for sure. I couldn't hear very well."

Bobby heard almost every member of his family start giggling. One of his cousins shouted, "You sound like Mr. McGillicuddy."

One of them shouted, *"Remember how you are al-ways telling us he says, 'What did you say'?"*

And all 25 bulbs in Bobby's family broke out laughing together.

"Did you say something? I keep hearing noises," shouted Mr. McGillicuddy.

That did it. Bobby made sure it got quiet inside the box. The snickers stopped, the giggling ended. It was silent. No reason to ever let the McGillicuddys know these bulbs were different from others. Talking bulbs? They would never believe that.

Of course, poor Mr. McGillicuddy would never figure out the noise came from inside the huge box which took both of his hands to hold as he picked it back up, balanced it against his chest, and walked to the opposite side of the room where the Christmas tree was waiting to be decorated.

And then, KERPLONK, down went the box, harder than before. It wasn't like Mr. McGillicuddy actual-ly dropped the box, but he never put it down gently either.

All the strands shook and the bulbs would lightly touch each other up above. But down where the Bright family strand lived, it hurt.

In fact, if you were at the bottom you got the worst of everything. During the daytime hours a small reflection of light would usually creep under the bottom of the closet door and could be seen by only those lucky bulbs and strands at the very top. That was the only light during the long months in the closet except for an occasional time when you might catch a glimpse of the sun's glow. But normally, there was little if any light past the halfway spot in the box. Certainly not any at the bottom where the Bright family ALWAYS spent the off season.

"*Ouch!*" Bobby's cousin Sparkling screamed. She began to cry and the bulbs next to her leaned over to see what happened.

"*It's okay, Sparkling,*" Bobby's Aunt Shining soothed. "*It's just a nick on the corner of your nose. You're still just as green as ever.*"

And then the wait began. Once the top of the box was folded back, the light poured in. Even for Christmas bulbs that can be a shocking experience after being in the dark for nearly 11 months. The light seemed way too bright for a moment, although that wasn't really so bad because at least there were things to see again.

"*Wow!*" Some of Bobby's aunt's and uncles were

whispering. *"This must be a real sunny day."* There was almost as much light at the bottom of the box as there was at the top.

Then the whispering stopped.

Everyone clearly heard Mrs. McGillicuddy.

"John, you test every strand this year. I don't want half the lights not working like last year." Her tone wasn't pleasant.

"Oh, there weren't that many that didn't work, Jane. Maybe a dozen at most."

"Just check them, John!"

As Bobby explained what had been said to his family, the testing began.

Mr. McGillicuddy removed the first strand of lights and moments later they heard the noise of the strand being "stretched out" on the floor.

"What did she say?" Bobby's dad whispered. In bulb language, Bobby whispered back, *"She's telling Mr. McGillicuddy he better check every bulb this year and replace them if they are dead."*

Bobby knew Mrs. McGillicuddy hadn't used the word "dead" but he also realized there was nothing sadder if you could no longer shine. For then there was no use for you, and soon you would be tossed in the trash and gone forever.

Last year Mr. McGillicuddy had gulped down his first big cup of eggnog before even starting to test the lights. The eggnog had obviously tasted good, because he consumed three more full cups and then he had fallen asleep. When he awoke he was definitely not in shape to "test" any more bulbs.

And thus, eleven of those "dead" bulbs were given an extra year with their families because Mr. McGillicuddy left the ones that were unlit on the strands. He never replaced them.

But this year was going to be different as Mrs. McGillicuddy had just made clear.

In a matter of a few minutes the "testing" began and even at the bottom of the box Bobby heard Mr. McGillicuddy shout, "Jane, where are the replacement bulbs? There are four lights out on this third strand."

For the next few minutes Bobby translated, as quickly as he could, the bad news to his family as they snuggled at the bottom of the box. The 10th and final strand waited to be tested so they could end up being placed at the back of the Christmas tree where they had spent nine straight years, with nobody ever getting to see them.

3

Danger for Bobby and His Family

Even though Mr. McGillicuddy always drank eggnog when he sorted through the strands of lights, it was too much to hope that he would drink too much for a second year in a row.

Mr. "Mac", as Bobby and the Bright family often referred to him, had only stopped twice to sip from the bright red mug filled with creamy thick apple cinnamon eggnog.

It was too bad, and sad too, for Mr. "Mac" had already put 12 non-working bulbs together in a pile in the corner when Bobby and his strand of lights were carried into the large game room.

Bobby saw for the first time the biggest tree he could ever remember in his ten years here. The corner of the room was completely covered by the branches of the giant noble fir.

"Oh, brother," Bobby whispered to his mom, "it's going to be the worst Christmas ever this year. No one looking at us, nothing to see, and our noses rubbing right up against the wall. There will hardly be room to get us on the back branches because the tree is so close to that wall."

Mr. "Mac" was using the hardwood floor area in front of the sofa at the opposite side of the room, rather than the soft Persian rug near the tree, to test the strands.

Usually when Mr. McGillicuddy tested on the rug he would just drop the bulbs onto the floor. Bobby re- membered that even on the soft rug it would hurt a little when you were dropped. But now, standing over the shiny floor, Mr. McGillicuddy dropped to a knee and gently placed the strand on the polished hardwood.

In most years, by the time Bobby's family was test- ed, Mr. McGillicuddy had either had too much eggnog to drink and didn't know what he was doing, or he was just tired from testing all the strands and wanted to start putting them on the tree.

But this year seemed different, Bobby thought, as Mr. McGillicuddy was very gentle with the bulbs as he placed them across the floor.

Bobby sighed and whispered to his mom and dad, *"Wouldn't it be wonderful if something different happened, and we didn't get stuck at the BACK of the tree. Oh to be lucky enough to be the last strand picked up and end up at the very front."*

But Bobby knew that wouldn't happen. The McGillicuddys were too well organized.

Bobby's Uncle Flicker started to say something but didn't get the chance. Mr. McGillicuddy clumsily brushed his foot against the strand as he walked away for another swig of eggnog and more than half of the strand bounced and twisted off the floor and onto the oriental rug.

"Ouch!" yelled one of Bobby's cousins. *"Hey, what's going on?"* shouted an aunt, as more gripes and screams were heard along the strand.

"Quiet, everyone," Bobby ordered in their magical "bulbese" language. Since he spoke and understood human language too, Bobby ran the show, even though there were times he wished he didn't have to.

Mr. "Mac" took a long gulp, and then waddled back and stared downward.

Bobby wondered if, even in his eggnog state of mind, Mr. McGillicuddy could ever imagine that he was looking at an entire family of bulbs. Bobby smiled as he looked up and down the strand at his parents, two sisters and a brother, two uncles and three aunts and a dozen cousins.

It just didn't seem fair, thought Bobby. Here we are. A special, different, amazing strand of lights, and we always get stuck at the back of the tree. All the other strands can't do anything but light up and shine when turned on.

But we can talk among ourselves. We are smart. And yet we always end up at the back of the tree where no one sees us, and we end up looking at that corner of the room with only one picture on the wall.

And then Bobby's thoughts returned to the moment. This was a nervous time every year. Would any of the lights fail to shine?

Would they "flicker" and "short out" as the McGilli-cuddys called it.

If it happened, there would be nothing to do but cry because Mrs. McGillicuddy set the rules and no partially working bulb would remain on her Christmas tree.

"No, John. Throw it out."

Bobby had heard those words enough times to know those bulbs that even fizzled slightly were gone for-ever and bingo, just like that, there was a new bulb in the socket.

Two years ago Bobby had lost a cousin next door and an uncle three sockets away.

Of course the replacement bulbs had none of the powers of the original Bright family and so as Bobby and his relatives would chatter from time to time when the room was empty, those two bulbs said nothing and understood nothing. In fact, the bulb that had replaced his uncle had actually been given the name of Uncle Radiant, even though he wasn't really a family member.

He got the name because Mr. "Mac" had accidentally dropped the bulb, chipping some of the natural orange coloring away, and leaving only a white glow from the top of his head.

Not that it really matters, thought Bobby. No one would see Radiant or any of the Bright family bulbs anyway.

"Here we go, son," his dad whispered.

Every bulb felt itself being lifted up. The plug was in Mr. "Mac's" hand. This was a special time. Work and you were on the tree, if not, you were in the trash.

As magical as Bobby and his family were, "sweating" was one human trait they did not have. If they had been able, he suspected that both the floor and rug would have been damp by now.

This was a dangerous time. A couple of cousins whispered *"ouch"* near the end of the strand as they bounced off the floor when Mr. McGillicuddy jiggled the plug.

For the first time in 47 weeks, Bobby and his relatives were about to feel the heat.

Later, as Christmas got closer, the McGillicuddy's would leave the lights on every night for five or six hours. By evening's end they would be very, very hot. But Bobby never minded how hot it got. After nearly 11 months locked up in that closet and turned off with no inside body heat, the warmth always felt good.

"Stand by, everyone," Bobby said. *"Here we go."*

And in procession type fashion each bulb would turn and say to the next, *"Here we go."*

Bobby knew that as fast as the message passed down the strand it was never quick enough to reach the relatives at the end before Mr. McGillicuddy would lift the plug and place it in the socket and "ZAP" on would come the lights. It was always a shocker for a split second if you hadn't been warned.

But in the end, a soft, almost noiseless cheer erupted. It was what Bobby's mom wisely called "our laughing expression of joy". And it was immediately followed by a top of the lungs shout of "YES" from Mr. McGillicuddy when he realized the lights were on. And then he'd repeat "YES" in his loud booming voice five or six more times.

However, today had been a little different. Mr. McGillicuddy had been calm and not once screamed "YES". Bobby had heard him quietly say "Okay" nine times. And even the six times there had been trouble he only said, "Uh, Oh! We've got some lights out."

That's why those bulbs were lying in the corner getting ready to disappear forever.

Suddenly Bobby realized he had been daydreaming and the strand had not been plugged in yet.

He listened for something to happen and thought, *"What difference does it make?"* The story was always the same.

Last out of the box, first on the tree, and then at the back where the Bright family's magical brightness was wasted on that old picture in the corner.

Suddenly he felt the strand jerk. This was the moment everyone anticipated. In a couple of seconds the plug would be inserted into the wall socket.

Bobby waited. And then he waited a little longer.

This was strange, he thought. There was no sound.

Uncle Flicker's warning had been passed all the way to the end of the strand and even Aunt Glaring had heard *"get ready."*

By now something should have happened. Bobby didn't like the sound of this, or in this case the fact there was no sound.

By now the heat should be shooting through 25 bulb bodies as they glowed for the first time in nearly 11 months.

It was the day after Thanksgiving and the time to cheer, if only for a few seconds when the "test" occurred and you began to shine.

But there was nothing.

"What's happening, Bobby?" timid little Blushing, Bobby's cousin two pods down whispered. Blushing hardly ever talked. She, like all the other bulbs, sensed something was wrong.

And then, instead of "yes", Mr. McGillicuddy screamed, "NO.....NO.....NO.....NO.....NO.....NO!"

It wasn't necessary to repeat it over and over. Once would have been enough. Bobby knew that one word— "NO"---meant trouble.

4

Bobby Takes a Chance

"**N**o! No! No! Not a whole strand," yelled Mr. McGillicuddy.

"What is it, John?"

Mrs. McGillicuddy came running into the room. She saw her husband standing there doing nothing. He only looked at the bulbs on the floor. No movement. Just a slight whimper.

"Are you alright, John?" Mrs. McGillicuddy shouted after she had twice nudged him with her arm.

"I'm okay. Yes. I'm okay."

Then he quickly added, "No, I'm not okay. Of course I'm not okay. Don't you see what I see?"

Mrs. McGillicuddy looked at the bulbs twisted like a snake stretching from the plug in the wall along the shiny hardwood floor in front of the sofa. She started to speak, but Mr. McGillicuddy just kept quietly mumbling to himself.

"Not the whole strand. Surely not every bulb is bad. I've already replaced at least a dozen bad bulbs on the other strands. I've never had that many go wrong, and now this."

And then he snapped loudly, "I may just throw the whole strand out."

"*No,*" screamed Uncle Glimmer. He didn't know but a few words of people talk, but he knew words like "throw" and "out" and Bobby had taught him how "go wrong" sounded when humans would say such things.

He lowered his voice even though he knew the Mc-Gillicuddys were too busy chattering about the strand that didn't work.

"*Find out if Bobby can hear them talking,*" he quickly told one of his sons, and down the strand like links in a chain came the whispers.

"*Ask Bobby if he can hear.*"

But Bobby had heard and before the question reached him he yelled back as loud as he could, "*Everyone, start twisting as hard as you can. Tighten up right now!*"

".....and you are not going to throw the whole string out," Mrs. McGillicuddy lectured her husband. "You wouldn't have 16 bulbs lying there if you hadn't drank all that eggnog last year and left all those dead ones on the tree."

Mr. McGillicuddy tried to argue. "There are only a dozen bad bulbs."

But that didn't work because Mrs. McGillicuddy snapped back, "No! Sixteen bulbs, John. I just counted them while you were standing there like a statue, mumbling and not moving. And quit putting the plug in and out of the socket. You're getting nothing done."

"Ouch that hurts!" The cries came from everywhere along the strand.

"What's wrong with that old man?" yelled Bobby's favorite cousin Energizer. *"He just cracked my nose. He scratched my sister's right side. She's chipped. Can't you do anything, Bobby?"*

But there was nothing Bobby could do. Mr. "Mac" pushed the plug in, and pulled it out at least five more times and nothing happened. There were no lights working. Not even one.

Bobby felt like the blame was his. If not, at least the guilt of knowing what Mr. McGillicuddy was saying. The other's didn't. If they did, he thought, they would be even more scared.

Bobby had promised himself he would never do again what he had learned three years ago, deep in the darkness of the storage box in the McGillicuddy's front closet. But this was a crisis. The end could be moments away.

It was times like this when Bobby wished he didn't understand human language, didn't know what was going on, and could be like everybody else.

But he knew it wasn't possible. He was different from all other Christmas tree light bulbs in the whole world. And because he was, and because he knew what was wrong, he would have to solve the problem by himself. Let's face it, he thought, this is definitely an emergency.

Especially when he heard Mrs. McGillicuddy's next words.

"That's it. No more messing around. I've changed my mind. Get rid of the whole strand. We'll just use the other nine this year unless you want to go buy another one."

Mrs. McGillicuddy stood across the room from her husband. He was on a knee near the wall socket making one last try, inserting and pulling out, and then again inserting and pulling out the plug.

"Are you listening, John?"

He wasn't. Poor Mr. McGillicuddy had slumped completely down to the floor and was sitting there leaning against the wall.

"John, did you hear me?"

But he said nothing. He had returned to that speechless daze of a few minutes ago, and he stood up and wandered over to one of the cane back swivel chairs at the kitchenette bar which divided the game room from the kitchen.

He sat down wearily and gazed back into the room. It was like he was staring at nothing as Mrs. McGillicuddy strode toward him snapping her hands. "Hello world. Are you there, Sir?" she kidded him.

"Yes, dear." Another mumble was followed by a big swig of eggnog from his red mug.

"Well, three more cups of that won't help you get things done, John McGillicuddy. Get on with this so we can put the lights on the tree. Into the trash can goes that whole strand and all those other bad ones too."

"What's happening? What's going on?"

The bulbs near Bobby were shouting but he was too busy. His mom and dad were watching in amazement as suddenly near the far end of the strand where they lived, they saw their son launch them and that part of the strand into the air as he yelled, *"ZERPLONK. ZER-PLONK. ZERPLONK!"*

His folks stared in amazement as Bobby chanted in a mysterious sounding voice those same words three more times. Then like magic, he twisted himself four times and fell free from his socket and onto the floor.

He lay there for a moment. Even he was shocked. It had worked. He had freed himself to do what he had to do.   And he knew if he didn't there would be no Bright family ever again.

5

Bobby Works His Magic

Mrs. McGillicuddy had left the room. Mr. "Mac" was still drinking his fourth cup of eggnog. He wouldn't be moving very fast now.

But Bobby knew he had to hurry because Mrs. Mc-Gillicuddy could make Mr. McGillicuddy move real fast if she barked at him like the McGillicuddy's dog Rocket often did.

Bobby rolled along the floor which he wished wasn't so shiny and hard because it was difficult to go quickly without making noise.

All he needed was to have Mr. "Mac" hear a bulb rolling on the floor and come see what was happening.

So he rolled to his left onto the carpet and picked up speed.

"*Quiet!*" is all he said as he passed relative after relative, each of them starting to say something, but only having time to look at him in amazement, as he whizzed on by them.

He continued to roll toward his goal which was the wall plug near the tree where Uncle Flicker and Aunt Shining dangled along with two of his cousins.

"How can you do that?" screamed his cousin Bingo.

"Shhh," whispered Bobby as he spun on past him.

"How did he get free?" asked another cousin, and the further along the floor he rolled, the more questions Bobby heard shouted.

Suddenly he stopped and looked back down the strand.

"SHHH, SHHH, SHHH," he said in an angry tone.

Didn't they know the danger they were in, he thought, as he continued toward the wall plug.

Of course they didn't, but he couldn't take time to tell them right now. That would frighten them even more if he suddenly stopped and told them they were all about to die.

Enough of this. Just do what you have to do, he thought, as he approached the edge of the rug. Now it was time to roll backward onto the floor again. He pointed his nose toward Mr. McGillicuddy so he could see clearly.

Across the room Mr. "Mac" sat there pouring himself his fifth mug of eggnog.

This was good, Bobby thought. He needed all the time possible, and another cup of eggnog would delay him from picking up the Bright family strand and throwing it away forever.

The biggest worry for Bobby now was whether he could do what he had planned. Having the ability to magically twist yourself free from your "chair" or "bed" or whatever you chose to call the individual socket you lived in was one thing.

To be able to make yourself roll across the floor was yet still another miracle. But now he knew his magical powers would be tested to the limit if his plan was going to work.

He looked up at his aunt and uncle as he inched toward the part of the strand which hung from the socket and was touching the floor.

Uncle Flicker was smart. He knew not to yell, even though Mr. McGillicuddy certainly wouldn't hear anything. In addition to guzzling more eggnog, Mr. "Mac" had started to sing Christmas songs.

"What are you doing, my brilliant nephew?" Uncle Flicker spoke quietly.

Bobby winked at his favorite uncle and smiled, but then quickly the smile vanished. Aunt Shining was hanging just below his uncle and tears were streaming down her nose.

"*Just help me,*" he whispered to his aunt.

"*What?*" she said and sniffled some more.

"*Why are you crying?*"

"*I'm scared for you. What are you doing?*"

"*Just watch.*" Bobby's face showed concern and his aunt looked straight at him. "*You'll see. I just need you to hold me when I get near you.*"

But then his aunt screamed as she stared in amazement. "*What are you doing? Are you crazy?*"

Bobby rolled on top of his new cousin Blinker and said, "*PUHRUMBA,*" as he sailed into the air, turned his nose and crashed into the twisted lines of the strand, falling right on top of Aunt Shining.

What she saw next left her speechless. She wasn't crying now. She was too shocked.

She watched in awe as her nephew sailed into the air again, shouted, "*PUHRUMBA!*"---and landed three more inches away at the very top of the strand, and squarely on the nose of her husband.

His uncle was so cool, Bobby thought. He said nothing. He just winked at me. Bobby leaned tightly against him so he wouldn't fall to the floor and for a brief moment thought about how much confidence his uncle had in him and how much confidence Bobby had in his Uncle Flicker.

Bobby remembered it had been during spring cleaning earlier this year.

Mr. "Mac" had lifted the box into the air to take it out of the closet and tripped and fell.

The Bright family strand buried at the bottom of the box had gotten turned inside out along with all the other strands above them and Bobby had found himself nose to nose with Uncle Flicker. They had spent the last seven months together with plenty to talk about.

It was during that time his uncle had told him he knew Bobby was really, really different from all the rest of the family and not just because he could understand human language.

Now Bobby hoped his uncle still thought he was that smart.

"Wish me luck, Uncle Flicker. We're all in trouble if this doesn't work."

What happened next made everyone know that Bobby was very, very, very special.

6

Bobby Puts His Plan to Work

Uncle Flicker watched in astonishment. With another *PUHRUMBA*, Bobby jumped away from his uncle and miraculously landed on top of the electrical plug at the end of the strand.

He teetered back and forth for a moment and came dangerously close to falling to the floor and smashing himself into eternity. But he was able to get control and once he did he clung to the wide end of the double pronged plug.

As he peered down to see the wall socket he wanted to cry with joy.

There were two different outlets in the socket as he had expected. Still you never knew until you saw it for yourself.

During his wild attempt to get the lights to work a few minutes ago, Mr. McGillicuddy had been pulling the plug from the wall, putting it in the lower socket and then pulling it out and putting it in the upper socket.

He had done this a number of times and Bobby figured there were two sockets, but had Mr. "Mac" been simply putting it in and pulling it out of the same socket, then his plan would have blown up in smoke.

And when Bobby thought of that he chuckled because that was just what he hoped his plan would do---blow everything up in smoke----and now there was a chance it could happen. He looked over the edge of the square green end of the plug as he held on tightly. It was a scary position to be in and Bobby was frightened.

He saw the floor below. He saw his speechless uncle staring up at him. Bobby wondered what it would be like to never see all of his family again. And he also wondered how much it would hurt if he hit the floor and shattered into tiny pieces.

"No time to think about this," Bobby scolded himself. *"Just do it or there's no hope anyway."*

From beneath his nephew, Uncle Flicker saw Bobby edge over the top of the plug's end, nearly slip and fall, and then at the last possible moment ram his bottom into the chain like cords which made up the strand.

At the very instant that Bobby was holding on for dear life, Mr. McGillicuddy on the other side of the room pushed aside the high kitchenette bar stool he had been sitting on and clumsily dropped his eggnog mug on the floor.

CRASH!

The mug broke into a jillion tiny pieces and scattered across the floor.

It was like a hailstorm. Eggnog mug chips were flying everywhere and the bulbs on the Bright family strand were ducking and twisting as most of the flying pieces missed. However, a few made contact.

Rocket started barking like mad from his room next to the kitchen.

Mr. "Mac" had put him there because the McGillicuddy's old dog loved to pull and chew on the bulbs and the cords when they were lying on the floor.

"What in the world was that?"

Bobby barely heard Mrs. McGillicuddy's voice from upstairs, but two seconds later he knew there was trouble because the CLUMP, CLUMP, CLUMP of her feet heading down the stairs left no doubt she was coming to make trouble for Mr. "Mac" and for Bobby if he didn't hurry.

He had to do it now. She would be in the room within seconds and even though she would chew out Mr. McGillicuddy and tell him to clean up the mess, she still might wander over near the tree. If she did she would most likely see a mysterious bulb laying on the strand near the socket.

"What have you done now?" she shouted and stormed into the room. Bobby couldn't wait any longer.

"PUHRUMBA." Bobby swung his gold threaded backside toward the two openings in the upper socket and jammed his rear end into one of the slits. With Mrs. McGillicuddy ripping into her husband and scolding him, Bobby had no worry about any noise being heard.

And the words PUHRUMBA, SCHNETTZ, and SCHNETTZ filled the air one more time.

The McGillicuddy's were yelling at each other and never heard the sizzle.

"SCHNETTZ," Bobby said it still one more time just to make sure his magical powers were in full gear. It had worked. From the outlet flew red and gold sparks, shooting downward toward the floor and looking very much like the closing moments of a sparkler as it burned out during a fourth of July celebration.

The bulbs along the strand who had been able to

twist into a position to see, watched Bobby in total awe. They couldn't believe it. Bobby had caused the wall socket to send sparks onto the floor. What in the world was he doing?

As they gaped at what was happening, Mrs. McGillicuddy was completely unaware as she continued to fuss and scold her husband.

"John, this is just too much. I go upstairs to put out the decorations for the guest room and you end up doing nothing but make a mess."

Even though Mrs. McGillicuddy's verbal attack on Mr. McGillicuddy continued, Bobby knew at any moment they might smell the smoke, see what the sparks had done, and even worse, see him hanging against the socket. He still had to hurry.

Now he managed to twist free from the intertwined cords in the strand and he fell downward landing on Uncle Flicker. But he had no time to talk and he quickly rolled onto Aunt Shining, then over both cousins and bounced down to the floor. His right side immediately started hurting.

He knew he was in trouble because as he started to roll towards the end of the strand his side already hurt more. He barely had the strength to roll over.

He had probably overdone this. His magical powers had managed to cause the electrical "short", but when it did it had taken almost all of his remaining energy.

He wasn't sure he could move any more until he heard the roar of Mrs. McGillicuddy's voice. That was reason enough to push onward.

"Go put Rocket outside so he will quit barking and get the broom and dust pan," Mrs. McGillicuddy ordered.

Bobby was trying but he slowed to a stop. He couldn't go on. He needed help. He was four bulbs from his "chair" but his energy was gone.

"I'll get a towel and wipe the eggnog up, and you John McGillicuddy, can pick up every piece of that broken mug. Then get rid of that strand and let's finish putting the good lights on the tree."

As exhausted as he was, when Mrs. McGillicuddy said those scary words, it was exactly what Bobby needed. He found a new level of energy. He was the only one who really understood the danger and if he didn't get going, he and all of his family were going to be picked up and thrown into the trash along with the broken pieces of an eggnog mug.

So with all of his might he started to roll again, and

as Rocket barked in the background, and Mr. and Mrs. McGillicuddy snipped at each other, Bobby's mom and dad, brothers and sisters cheered as he rolled once, twice, three, four, five, six, seven times, and finally on the eighth roll they saw him, through their wide open eyes, magically twist back into his "chair" socket. *"PUHRUMBA,"* he spun forward four times and locked himself tightly in.

Now it was up to the plan. Would it work?

7

Look What Bobby Did

Mr. McGillicuddy took 15 minutes searching the floor and picking up pieces of his eggnog mug before he was certain there were no more.

Mrs. McGillicuddy checked the floor and both rugs in the game room and agreed everything had been found.

But they were both wrong. One of Bobby's cousins, Whitening, who had gotten her name because she was a white bulb with scratches on both sides, had been hit by one of the pieces of the broken mug and it lay underneath her along with a big drop of eggnog that had splashed squarely on her nose.

Because she was so sparkling silver with all of those scratches, Mr. "Mac" did not see the eggnog or the small piece of mug.

"I'm sure I got every broken piece, Jane."

Mrs. McGillicuddy sighed and headed out the door.

"Alright then, throw everything out. I'm going back upstairs to finish decorating the guest room."

"Oh no!" Bobby gulped.

"What is it, son?" his mom whispered.

Bobby knew none of his family knew of the danger. He just knew his plan was either going to work within the next couple of minutes or it would be all over.

"Not now, mom. Just hope for the best."

Before his mom could answer, Bobby heard Mrs. Mc-Gillicuddy open the double doors leading into the living room. As she stepped down into the room she yelled back to her husband, "Our little Remington is going to enjoy that tiny Christmas tree we bought for him. He'll be one happy little grandson when he sees all the lights and decorations."

Mr. McGillicuddy was out of it. Between a broken mug, strands of lights on the floor, some working and others not, plus his wife screaming at him every few minutes, he didn't have a clue what was going on. "What did you say, honey?"

"What's wrong with you today, John? Don't you listen to anything I say?"

"Yes, dear. It's just...I mean I know you're putting up the little tree upstairs. I heard that. It's just...

I can't believe everything that's gone wrong. I don't remember the wall plug looking like this," he said, and bent down on his knees to get a closer look.

"Oh my gosh! Look at this. Did I do that?"

"Now what, John?" she said, and like a charging bull jumped back into the game room and raced to see what her husband was staring at.

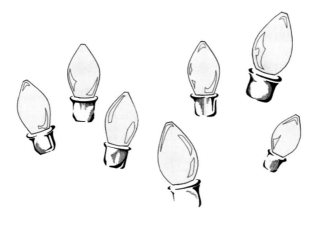

8

Bobby's Plan Saves the Family

Bobby held his breath. He looked toward the wall socket. Even though none of his family understood what he had tried to do, he was sure they knew something important was happening.

Just as Mrs. McGillicuddy reached her husband, he raised up from his kneeling position to yell at her and the two bumped heads.

"Ouch! Be careful. That hurt. What's wrong, John?"

"I didn't do this. I promise. I didn't do anything."

Mrs. McGillicuddy took one quick look and knew what had happened. At least she thought she did.

"You've blown a fuse or something. It looks like a fire burned the wall plate cover. Look at those burn marks. What did you do?"

Before he could answer, Mrs. McGillicuddy was interrupting and yapping some more. No chance for Mr.

"Mac" to get a word in edgewise.

"We'll have to call Stan. Phone him right now and tell him to get over here. Okay?"

"We can't put the strands on the tree if none of them are going to light. We may have to put in a new electrical system in the whole room." She stopped to catch her breath before the orders quickly continued. "I said call Stan right now."

Mr. "Mac" staggered to his feet in a daze. His eyes and expression told it all.

With a look of confusion, he stared first at the burned wall plate, then at the strands of lights across the floor, and the growing collection of dead bulbs in the corner. Everything was a mess and his wife kept screaming.

Finally, he had enough.

"What are you talking about? Stan Jones is not working the day after Thanksgiving. He's watching the football game right now. That you can be assured. And he doesn't plan to open the store this weekend."

Mr. McGillicuddy liked this. He was doing the talking. His wife was actually listening.

"You know my brother-in-law isn't getting out of that ugly old chair of his to come over here and look at a wall socket. He won't do anything about it or anything else until all those football games are over on Sunday."

Mrs. McGillicuddy slumped down onto the thick leather couch, grabbed a couple of pillows and put them against her stomach and bent over like she was in pain. She listened to her husband carry on about her brother and his football games.

As she stared back at the mess, her eyes focused on the far end of the strand on the floor.

"I think she's looking at me," Bobby said quietly to his parents. "It's like she knows something."

"What have you done, Bobby?" his mom whispered.

"I broke the wall socket, mom." That was enough to say. Trying to explain about electric current and electricity was too confusing. He knew his family wouldn't understand.

It wasn't because they were dumb. They were the only Christmas tree lights in the whole world that could talk with each other.

But Bobby was just plain smarter. It didn't make him better than the other bulbs in his family, but there was no doubt he was the most unique bulb in a family of different bulbs.

It was because of this special talent of understanding human language, that at this very moment he knew his gamble had paid off.

Mrs. McGillicuddy jumped up, pushed her husband aside and said, "Give me this strand right now."

She reached down and pulled the plug free. "I'm taking this strand upstairs and see if it will work. You throw out those loose bad bulbs and I don't care what football game is on TV. You call Stan and tell him to be here tomorrow morning."

And with that she swept up the lights from the floor and with the strand bundled in her arms, headed out of the room. "I'm going to get <u>something</u> done today."

"*What's happening?*" Everyone was screaming. Cousins who had only seen each other from a distance were all twisted together against one another as Mrs. McGillicuddy tromped through the living room, with about half of the bulbs bouncing over the floor.

Bobby and his folks were lucky. They had ended up in Mrs. McGillicuddy's arms, face to face with Uncle Flicker and Aunt Shining, sort of like during the spring cleaning fiasco when Mr. "Mac" had dropped the box and everyone had gotten tossed around.

"*Bobby, what have you done? Where are we going? Aren't we going to be on the back of the tree?*"

Bobby had no time to answer. He was being jostled like everyone else.

Mrs. McGillicuddy reached the staircase and before heading upstairs picked up two boxes of ornaments sitting on a hall table. She stuck the boxes between her left arm and her plump waist. The bulbs flew over her shoulders and tumbled down her back.

"Ouch!"

"That hurts!"

"You're hitting me."

"Well, you're hurting me."

"I'm squashed. I can't see anything."

Bobby tried with little luck to get them quiet. Didn't make any difference because they weren't going to be heard while Mrs. McGillicuddy ascended the stairs.

CLOMP, CLOMP, CLOMP.

"Be quiet. We're definitely not going outside now. She's headed up the stairs."

"It's going to be Okay!" Bobby shouted. He knew two things. One, they were not being thrown away because he knew the lights would work if they were plugged into the wall socket upstairs. And two, the Bright family was going to have its greatest Christmas ever.

He wasn't sure how it would happen, but he just knew

it would.

He whispered to his mom and dad as Mrs. McGillicuddy dropped the tangle of bulbs onto the bed in the upstairs bedroom. *"I've got good news."*

PART TWO

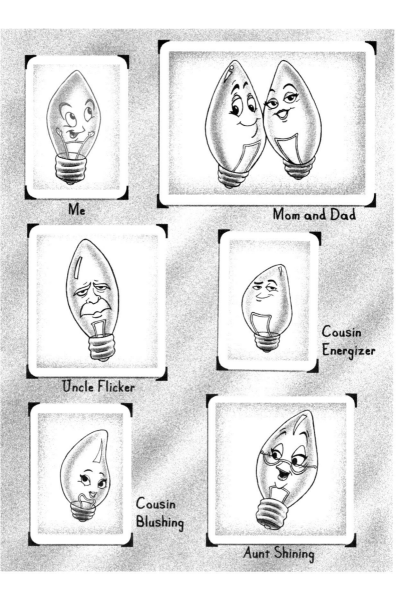

Me

Mom and Dad

Uncle Flicker

Cousin
Energizer

Cousin
Blushing

Aunt Shining

9

Two Weeks Before Christmas

Bobby and the other 24 bulbs in the Bright family lay intermingled among the branches of the tiny Christmas tree sitting on the table in the corner of the McGillicuddy's upstairs bedroom.

It was Sunday morning at 11 o'clock when Bobby heard the garage door open.

Mr. and Mrs. McGillicuddy were returning from early church service and would be busy from the moment they entered the house.

This was the day for a huge party they had every year which they called the "Big One".

Even though the Bright family was happier than they had ever been, they were just a little lonely without the other strands that decorated the big tree downstairs.

But it was still okay. For the first time in their life they were not looking at a wall in the corner of a room, hidden from view of everyone, just lying there and not even really existing. This was "fun" because even if Mr. and Mrs. McGillicuddy only came upstairs occasionally, at least they saw the bulbs. It was good to be appreciated for the first time in your life.

Every bulb had something to see as they horizontally and vertically crisscrossed the front of the small scotch pine from top to bottom. They could see the bed, the chairs, the television, and the fancy Lladro figures that graced the book shelves in the far corner.

All of this had happened because of Bobby's magical powers and heroics two weeks ago. Bobby knew they were very lucky things had worked out the way they did in those hectic minutes when they could have been tossed in the trash. He and his family had chatted in "bulbese" many times about the moment that had changed their lives on that fateful evening the day after Thanksgiving.

It would be remembered forever. Mrs. McGillicuddy had scooped up the strand, stormed up the stairwell with half the bulbs in her arms and the rest of the strand alternately bouncing off the side of her leg and the stairs as she jostled her way to the guest room at the top.

Bobby smiled as he thought back to the moment. Mrs. McGillicuddy CLOMP, CLOMP, CLOMPING up the stairs and all the bulbs holding their breath and whispering to Bobby, *"What is happening?"*

Bobby smiled, remembering he didn't have a clue what was happening. He tried to act brave. *"Take it easy. Everything is going to be fine,"* he had said, not really knowing if that was true.

Amazingly though, everything turned out even more than fine. In fact, it was wonderful.

Instead of being tossed in the trash they now had their very own tree and for the most part their very own room.

But it had been a close call and Bobby smiled again as he thought back to the moment Mrs. McGillicuddy had entered the room.

She had started at the top and quickly wrapped the strand back and forth across the front of the tree stretching it toward the bottom. When she realized there were still a few bulbs at the end of the cord she had started to place those remaining ones, including Bobby, his mom and dad, and brother and sister at the back of the tree.

"Not again!" Bobby recalled crying out. *"Not at the back of another tree."*

His mom had started crying. *"Will we ever get to shine for anyone?"*

It was then something very "lucky" happened. The telephone rang, just as Bobby was whining, his mom was crying and Mrs. McGillicuddy was reaching to place the remaining bulbs at the back of the tree.

Before she could do that, the phone rang loudly a second time from Mr. McGillicuddy's upstairs office, which was just around the corner from the guest room. Mrs. McGillicuddy had stretched the strand tightly and had started to place the bulbs at the back of the tree when the phone rang a third time. She paused for a moment, and muttered to herself, "That man never answers a phone." Then, she dropped the rest of the strand into a small straight back chair sitting next to the tree and raced to Mr. McGillicuddy's office to answer the phone which was now ringing for a fifth time.

Bobby, laying flat on the chair, had looked up at the bulbs dangling down the side of the tree.

"It's over isn't it, Bobby?" It was his dad and he was

sobbing. Bobby recalled the moment so clearly. It was another of his great achievements and he couldn't help but smile.

"*No, dad.*" Bobby had shouted. "*It's not over.*"

And just like that, Bobby had put his magical powers to work again.

"*ZERPLONK. ZERPLONK!*" he had shouted, and then just to be sure he had shouted one more time, as loud as he could---"*ZERPLONK.*"

WHOOOSH..... Bobby and the rest of the bulbs dangling from the tree, plus those lying on the chair, all flew right up to the front branches where they had landed on top of some of the other bulbs. Shouts had come from his family. "*What's going on? What are you doing on top of me? Are you crazy Bobby?*"

Bobby replied, "*Just wait a little bit.*"

With the help of two more *PUHRUMBAS* and a *ZERPLONK* he managed to twist the rest of the strand neatly toward the top of the tree letting the remaining bulbs drop downward into the middle.

It had been even more magical than getting up to the tree.

And just to make sure he really had his amazing powers working, he twisted himself so he was perched right at the very center of the tree.

He felt selfish about being right in the middle, but only a little bit. The most important thing was every bulb on the strand could see all of the room.

The rest of the bulbs had cheered and cheered.

Bobby still got a little "sweaty" thinking about how lucky they had been. Just moments after the strand had been successfully stretched across the front of the tree, Mrs. McGillicuddy's footsteps rattled across the floor.

"Quiet, I hear her coming," he yelled sharply.

Walking back toward the bedroom Mrs. McGillicuddy yelled down the staircase, "Dwight, Jan, Suzette, and Bruce will be a couple of hours late."

When she entered the bedroom she yelled one more time, "Did you hear me, John?"

Bobby felt the anxiety as the bulbs all held their breath.

She bent down to pick up the bulbs she had hurriedly dropped on the chair.

Bobby remembered how frightened he was at the moment.

Mr. McGillicuddy's voice echoed up the stairwell, "What did you say?"

"I'll tell you in a minute," she had shouted back.

"What did you say?" Mr. McGillicuddy had yelled again.

"Not now, I'll tell you in a minute," she had screamed once more.

Every bulb stared at Mrs. McGillicuddy, and even though they couldn't understand, they knew this was THE moment. Would she realize the bulbs had moved by themselves?

But it was then, another of those special miracles took place.

"Have I lost my mind? I didn't put all those bulbs on the tree did I?"

She had stood there for a moment muttering to herself, before putting her hands on her hips and looking around the room, as if maybe someone else was also there. Finally, she had peered around to the back of the tree where she didn't see any bulbs. She then shook her head and said loudly, "I surely must be losing my memory."

With that statement, she turned and walked out of the room and down the stairs. Two seconds later everyone had sighed with relief and cheered softly.

The bulbs laughed in unison when Bobby told them

Mrs. McGillicuddy's final words: "I know I didn't put all of those bulbs on the front of that tree."

Now Bobby stared straight ahead. His thoughts of that fortunate moment two weeks ago made him feel good, because he knew for certain that this was going to be the greatest Christmas ever for him and his family.

And here's what happened.

10

Let the Party Begin

Bobby and every member of the Bright family would remember the moment forever. The clock above the bed straight across from the small Christmas tree read 3:15 p.m. when Mrs. McGillicuddy came back into the room, reached down and put the plug in the wall socket and hurried right out of the room and back downstairs.

As she disappeared, the whole family cheered and put on their brightest smiles. They winked, laughed and enjoyed the moment. Bobby explained to them that they needed to shine brighter than ever before, because a lot of people were going to be coming upstairs to play the different games the McGillicuddy's always had at their party.

Guests would be wandering through the rooms laughing, talking and enjoying the party, and when they were in the guest room they would be looking at the beautiful lights.

Finally Bobby and his family were going to make people happy after nine straight years of being hidden out of sight.

Bobby wished Mrs. McGillicuddy would have looked at the tree lights before racing out of the room. Would she have realized how much brighter the bulbs appeared? Probably not, he thought. Her mind was elsewhere. It should have been because 15 minutes later the doorbell rang for the first of many times as the guests started to arrive.

11

It's Party Time

It was a night to remember and for as long as they were together the Bright family would talk of this evening when they got to shine for more than 50 people.

Bobby was one busy bulb as people walked in and out of the guest room waiting their turns to play games in the other rooms upstairs.

"What are they saying?"

"Why are they pointing?"

"Look at that big face looking at me!"

Every bulb was chattering away in silent bulb language and Bobby with his magical powers was translating what the humans were saying.

"He just said he never saw such bright lights in his life."

"She just said this was the prettiest little tree she

had ever seen."

"That big face told the other woman it was because the lights are so bright."

That's the way it went all night long. Hardly anyone entered the room without saying something about the bright lights and the pretty little tree.

It was a miracle and some of Bobby's aunts just couldn't help but cry. All the bulbs were so happy.

"Look at all the people looking at us."

"We can be seen."

"We are doing what we were made to do."

"We're making the room bright."

"We're making the room shine."

"We're making all these people smile."

For a moment Bobby thought Aunt Shining would never quit talking. She was so excited. But then he thought, why shouldn't she be? This was what their life was all about, making people happy.

"We're going to shine every night through Christmas," Bobby predicted.

When all the party goers took a break to go downstairs for dinner, Bobby and his family had their own little party breaking into chorus to sing a song Bobby had taught them.

"We're gonna shine all Christmas season,
We're gonna shine every night.
We're gonna shine, shine, shine,
And be very, very bright."

That's just what happened as the party continued into the evening.

When the last guest left just before 11 o'clock, the Bright family relaxed and rested, and soon Mr. McGillicuddy wandered upstairs and unplugged the lights.

Bobby whispered to the others, "Get a good night's sleep. We are going to be busy shining brightly."

He couldn't have been more wrong as they were soon to find out.

12
Night Time December 23rd

No one spoke any longer. What was there to say? Bobby and his family felt like they did during those long months waiting for the spring cleaning break and the even longer wait until Thanksgiving.

All the excitement of the night of the McGillicuddy's annual Christmas party had ended as quickly as it had begun.

Now 15 days after the moment when Bobby and his family had been the happiest Christmas tree light bulbs in the entire world, things were just like they had been all those other years.

They weren't stuck in the back of the tree downstairs, but they might as well have been. Nothing. A big nothing had happened since the party. Not once had the lights been turned on.

Bobby was disappointed and so were all the other

bulbs, but Bobby knew he had to keep everyone's spirits up.

The way to do that was to tell the story again of what had happened after the party was over.

Mr. and Mrs. McGillicuddy had come upstairs to turn off the tree lights.

When they entered the room they stopped and held hands.

Bobby smiled to himself as he thought about it and said to all the bulbs, *"Okay guys, let's cheer up a little bit and think about that famous moment again."*

Not every bulb was ready to play old memories though. Some were tired of hearing or remembering the same old story. But what choice did they have? Might as well think of the good times, and still be happy that they weren't stuck at the back of the big tree.

So Bobby told the story again of Mrs. McGillicuddy hugging her husband and saying, "It was a great party, John."

"Yes it was, dear," Mr. McGillicuddy had said as they sat down on the bed together. "I can't believe how many people told me these were the brightest lights they had ever seen on a Christmas tree. I mean lights are lights. You would have thought they had some magical power the way everyone talked. I think a bunch of people had too much eggnog."

Bobby and most of the bulbs laughed when Bobby recounted that moment and Bobby tried to talk like Mr. McGillicuddy. In fact, Bobby played the parts of everyone whenever he told a story.

The sadness was wearing off and the bulbs were starting to get excited again as Bobby recounted the tale of that wonderful evening.

"I'm sure you're right about that, dear," Mrs. McGillicuddy had giggled and then added, "yourself included."

"Well at least I didn't go around telling people that these lights looked like they were smiling at me. There must have been ten people tell me something that silly."

Bobby smiled as he remembered the very moment Mr. McGillicuddy had made that comment. Rocket had raced upstairs and as the McGillicuddy's dog slid into the guest room, he bumped the tree, nearly knocking it over.

"Oh my gosh," Mrs. McGillicuddy had screamed. "Watch what you're doing Rocket! But Rocket had more to say and he barked and barked and barked some more.

The more Mrs. McGillicuddy yelled, "Stop barking," the more Rocket had barked.

And through all of the action Mr. McGillicuddy just sat there and stared at the tree, his mouth wide open.

Bobby giggled as he told the story.

"What is it?" his mom asked.

"Oh I was just thinking about the look on Mr. McGillicuddy's face when he saw all of us smiling after Rocket bumped the tree."

Bobby's mom started to giggle too. Then his dad also laughed.

"What's going on, Bobby?" Uncle Flicker shouted.

"Just thinking about old Mr. McGillicuddy and that weird look on his face when he saw all of us smiling at him." Uncle Flicker started to laugh, and then Aunt Shining, and suddenly every bulb on the tree was giggling.

"Tell it again, Bobby," one of his cousins yelled down to him from the other end of the strand at the top of the tree.

And now that he had everyone's attention, Bobby continued his one-bulb show, playing both roles and re-living the hilarious moment.

"Jane, those bulbs are smiling. They really are smiling at me."

"John McGillicuddy, don't you drink another ounce of eggnog again. You are just too silly."

"*He looked like a statue,*" Bobby's cousin Dazzling interrupted.

"*Yes, he did,*" someone else said and then all the bulbs laughed some more and the branches on the tiny tree shook as the laughter continued.

Everyone was happy again if only for the moment.

It was a half hour since the laughter had finally ended and now the branches shook no more. The bulbs lie quiet among them.

It was nearly midnight and Bobby knew Christmas Eve was only moments away. Had all this been worth it? he wondered. Had he saved everyone so they could have only one night to make people happy?

Being upstairs alone was tough. Even in all those other years, staring at the back wall downstairs, at least you heard the McGillicuddy's talking, heard the television, and the Christmas music playing.

And Bobby knew those other strands didn't have his family's magical powers, so they couldn't even understand or appreciate all those things. It just wasn't fair.

Bobby felt the tug and turned. His mom had shook herself inside her pod and Bobby turned to her.

"Bobby, don't try to understand everything and don't gripe so much."

Suddenly, Bobby realized he had been talking to himself. He started to say something, but his mom continued, *"We've finally had some happy times. Be thankful we've at least made people happy for a few hours. And besides,"* she added, "maybe our biggest moment is still ahead."

"You heard Mrs. McGillicuddy say her grandson was coming for Christmas. She said that was the reason for this Christmas tree being here. Don't you quit believing Bobby, I think we've got some big bright moments in front of us."

Bobby smiled at his mom's pun just as the clock in the front hallway downstairs struck midnight.

Now it was quiet. The McGillicuddy's were asleep, the tree lights in the big room downstairs were turned off.

Bobby sat perched at the front of the tiny tree upstairs wondering if his mom could possibly be right.

"*Can it really happen?*" he spoke quietly to himself.

But no one heard. All the other bulbs were sleeping as Bobby muttered, "*Am I the only one who really
cares?*"

13

Christmas Eve Afternoon

It was quiet. No one spoke in the Bright family as they lay twisted throughout the branches of the tiny scotch pine. The few moments of laughter last night now forgotten.

They stared at the empty guest room knowing full well that even though it was daytime, the lights on the tree downstairs were all turned on and glowing.

Mrs. McGillicuddy only turned on the tree lights at night until the day before Christmas. But on Christmas Eve she turned them on when she first got out of bed in the morning. If she opened the shutters in the big room to let the sunlight shine inside, she still kept the lights turned on. It was a McGillicuddy tradition.

"Christmas tree lights should always shine all Christmas Eve and Christmas day," Bobby had heard Mrs. Mc-Gillicuddy say every year.

Bobby remembered those earlier years. Even if they only shined toward a bare wall at least they were doing something. That's what was happening downstairs with the other bulbs, but it wasn't happening upstairs.

Suddenly the doorbell rang. Rocket barked and raced to the front door.

"Be quiet, Rocket," Mrs. McGillicuddy screamed. "Don't get so excited." And then Bobby heard Mr. McGillicuddy, who had been working in his office nearby, CLOMP, CLOMP, CLOMP down the stairs.

"Come on, John, the kids are here. Let's open the door together."

Bobby heard the door lock turn and the white plaque with the goofy looking old goat and a funny message on it, which hung on the front door, rattled loudly as the heavy wooden front door was pulled open.

Just before the glass door that was in front of the main door opened and all the hugs, shouts, laughter, kisses, barking and other things that took place when relatives arrived for Christmas began to happen, Bobby's mom leaned toward him and whispered, *"Mark this time down. I think we'll remember it forever."*

Bobby looked at the clock next to the bed. It read 2:15 p.m., December 24th.

First the luggage was brought from the car while Remington and his grandparents toured the house.

At seven years of age Remington still wasn't tired of seeing the bedroom where his father had slept as a boy. He always liked to look at some of the high school basketball awards his dad had won. Trophies were everywhere, and Remington's dad had promised him he could have them when he was older.

Every Christmas, Remington would ask Mrs. McGillicuddy, "Grandma, can I take those trophies home?"

And she would always say, "Ask your daddy. But I think he wants you to be older when you take them."

"Please, grandma?" Remington would ask, and then before she could answer he would race away shouting, "I want to see the tree."

It was the same way this year. Bobby heard Remington running and figured there would be no more talk about trophies during the next three days.

In the past, it had been much easier for Bobby to hear Remington talking to the McGillicuddys but this year was different being upstairs. Bobby strained to listen, but it was too difficult and he could only imagine what it had been like in recent years.

Remington would probably be shouting excitedly at this very moment as he raced into the game room.

Bobby imagined the little freckle faced redhead jumping up and down and shouting what he had always said since he was old enough to talk, "Oh boy, do the bulbs look big this year and are they ever bright."

Bobby smiled as he thought of what Remington had said every year, "Are these new bulbs, grandma?"

And Bobby could see Mrs. McGillicuddy turning and smiling. "Lisa, he says the same thing every year." And then they both would laugh.

And sure enough, downstairs that very conversation was taking place.

"Well, they look bigger," Remington frowned and stuck his nose down close to the bulbs nestled in the middle of the big tree. "Are you sure, Grandma?"

"I'm sure," Mrs. McGillicuddy chuckled. "But is that all you're interested in? What about the presents?"

"What presents?" Remington asked. "Where?

Where are they?" he screamed.

"You mean you don't remember?" His mom smiled and winked at her mother-in-law.

"What's going on here?" Mr. McGillicuddy asked as he and Remington's dad walked into the room.

"Where are the presents, dad?" Remington asked as he raced to his father who stood with his hands facing upward and a look of disbelief on his face.

"You mean you don't know?"

"No. But you do, don't you? Granddaddy told you, didn't he, dad?"

"Remington, you say the same thing every year. Ever since you were, what Lisa, maybe three years old, he's said the same thing."

"That's right," Remington's mom smiled, "the very same thing. Think for a minute Remington. Where do grandma and granddaddy put the presents before we put them under the tree?"

Remington stood looking at his mom, hands on hips and very puzzled. He pushed his right index finger up against his nose and thought.

Mrs. McGillicuddy started to laugh and so did everyone else.

Suddenly Remington shouted, "The closet upstairs!

I remember. Am I right? Are they there?"

"Is this December 24th?" Remington's dad laughed and looked at his parents. "Some things never change."

"And some things should never change, Richard," Mrs. McGillicuddy added.

"What do you mean, grandma?" Remington asked.

"Never mind. Let's just get upstairs and find some presents."

Remington started to race out of the room but his grandpa reached and grabbed him.

"Hold on, little guy. This year there is something even better than presents upstairs."

"I doubt that," Mrs. McGillicuddy said, "but pretty close."

"What? What is it?" Remington shrieked. He was bouncing up and down, and jumping back and forth like some crazy out of control spinning top. It was something Remington always did when he got excited, and he was really excited now.

"Let's go see," Remington's grandparents said in unison and winked at their confused looking grandson.

"But when you get to the top of the stairs you have to close your eyes."

"Mom, what have you guys done?" asked Remington's

dad.

"You'll see."

And with that the five of them headed to the staircase.

"They just said keep your eyes closed," Bobby said in a low voice.

"And Mrs. McGillicuddy just told Remington there were only a few more steps to a big surprise."

Bobby's mom twisted herself toward Bobby. *"I think we're about to become very important, Bobby."*

Bobby started to say something, but Mr. McGilli-cuddy burst into the room. "Now stay right there Remington and keep those eyes closed. Only four more steps to go."

And then he reached down and grabbed the plug and plunged it into the socket. As the prongs made contact the Bright family strand did what it did best. Every light smiled and shined immediately and the tiny Christmas tree stood there glowing brightly, ready to make the mouth of a little boy named Remington open wide.

The sun's rays forced themselves through a tiny

opening in the shutters of the window directly opposite the tree, as if to battle for the spotlight, but Bobby and his family were too much of a match. They shined brighter than they ever had, including the night of the big party, and the sun's rays had no chance to win this battle.

"Let's be the brightest Christmas tree lights ever," Bobby shouted without fear of being heard. Mr. McGillicuddy was back in the hall where there was more loud chattering and laughter. And above all the voices was Remington's yelling, "What's going on?" as he bounced up and down as if he was jumping on a pogo stick.

"Go in and see," Mrs. McGillicuddy shouted.

And then all the giggling and talking stopped in unison. He entered the room with the eyes of his parents, grandparents, and every Christmas tree bulb staring at him.

His mouth opened wide, but no sound came out. His two blue eyes appeared to be as large as coffee cups, and his strawberry blonde hair looked like it was standing straight up on the top of his head.

It was a sight to see.

The Bright family had focused every ray of light they could muster upon Remington who stood in the doorway in a spotlight of red, white, blue, orange, and green colors.

Those sun rays never had a chance. It was as if the room was dark except for the tree lights.

The clock read 2:35 p.m., December 24th and Bobby knew none of his family would ever forget the time.

14

Remington Meets New Friends

The noise never stopped from the moment Remington squealed, "Oh my gosh! A Christmas tree in mom and dad's room."

"That's right, Remington, except this is your room this year."

"What's going on?" Remington's mom asked as the oohs and aahs continued around the room.

"I think the lights are brighter than any we've ever had."

"Oh John, you always say that," Mrs. McGillicuddy said as she looked at her husband who stood there with his mouth as wide open as his grandson's had been just moments ago.

"No. I mean it," Mr. McGillicuddy said.

Remington's mom asked, "Will you guys tell me what's going on?"

"Of course, dear," Mrs. McGillicuddy smiled. "This is Remington's room this Christmas."

"It is?" Remington screamed. "You mean it, grandma!"

"It sure is."

And while Mrs. McGillicuddy explained what was planned for Remington, he and his folks listened and did not notice what happened next.

"*Let's be ornery!*" Bobby shouted to his family. And that was all he had to say because the bulbs had discussed what would happen if Remington was going to stay in this room during the Christmas visit.

"She means it, little guy," said Mr. McGillicuddy and he reached down and picked up Remington.

The bulbs had all shifted slightly throughout the branches of the tiny tree and now were focusing every ray of light they could muster on the jabbering little redhead in the arms of his granddad.

The two stood together in a multicolored spotlight.

"Your mom and dad are sleeping in the new big bed in your dad's old room."

"What happened to the little bed?" Remington asked.

"You mean you didn't notice the new bed when you were looking at daddy's trophies?" Mrs. McGillicuddy smiled.

"Nope. I didn't even notice," Remington said and quickly asked, as if he still wasn't sure, "so this is my own tree?"

"Your own tree for a big 7-year old who can lay here at night and watch the lights until you go to sleep."

"Yeah!" Remington screamed and then his mouth flew open.

"Granddaddy. Look! We're in the spotlight. Look! The lights are shining on us. And the bulbs love me," he said, pointing his finger toward the tree. "They are all smiling."

And everyone laughed as Remington waved at the bulbs.

His mom did too, but as she stood inside the doorway chuckling, a puzzled look crept over her face.

"Honey," she said to Remington's dad, "it really does look like a spotlight."

"Are you crazy?" Remington's dad answered.

"No. Really. Come here in the doorway and look. It's weird."

"Puhleez, Lisa."

"No, dad! Mom's right. I can feel the spotlight. It's in my eyes."

Then Mrs. McGillicuddy and her son both laughed and before Remington's mom could say another word, Remington jumped down from his granddad's arms and raced to the front of the tree to touch and feel the lights.

"Ouch! They are hot."

"You be careful. Don't be touching those bulbs," his mom scolded.

"Okay, mom, but they really are smiling," Remington said.

And Mr. McGillicuddy nodded. "You know, you're right, Remington. They do look like they're smiling."

"Sure, dad," Remington's father said to Mr. McGillicuddy. "And you've been in the eggnog while you were waiting for us to get here."

Then all the adults laughed, but Remington never turned his head.

His eyes looked even larger.

"That one bulb winked at me," he screamed.

And then his parents and grandparents burst out into more laughter.

"No, I mean it," he insisted.

When they all laughed one more time, Remington turned to try and explain exactly what he had seen.

As Remington tried to convince his parents, Bobby leaned against his dad and whispered, *"Remington just saw me smile and wink at him."*

"You be careful you don't get us in trouble."

"Just two little boys having fun, dad."

"Wait a minute," Remington suddenly screamed, "I thought we were coming up here to find some presents."

"Yes we are," Mr. McGillicuddy shouted, "starting right now," and he reached into the closet and pulled out a huge present decorated with Santa Claus wrapping paper and featuring a big red bow with two large bells that tinkled as he dragged it into the room.

And with that the Bright family's greatest Christmas ever got into full swing.

15

Remington Talks.
Bobby Listens.

There would be more Christmas seasons and they would be wonderful.

Bobby was sure of that. But he also knew that this would be the most special. At least, at the moment he thought it would be.

How could anything be better? If it got any better than this year it would be unbelievable.

Remington spent every moment he could in his "own" room with his "own" tree and he and the bulbs became great friends.

They talked all the time. Well at least Remington talked. Bobby wanted to so badly. However, he couldn't say another word because just like Remington had to mind his dad, Bobby must mind his father too.

"Don't you even think about it," his dad had yelled

at him while the McGillicuddys, Remington, and his mom and dad were having Christmas Day dinner.

"*Oh, dad, think how much fun it would be,*" Bobby said.

"*You be careful,*" his mom chimed in. "*This has been a wonderful Christmas. Don't go and do something to make the McGillicuddys think that little boy shouldn't have his own tree.*"

"*Oh, Mom! Get real. Do you think they would really believe him if he told them a Christmas tree bulb had talked to him?*"

"*You never know,*" Bobby's mom had said cautiously. "*You just never know.*"

What Bobby did know was that if he had his chance and could do it without getting caught, then he would.

"*I know I have great magical powers,*" Bobby thought to himself, "*I just know I could get him to understand me.*"

16
Bobby Reminisces

Remington jumped out of bed the day after Christmas and into an upstairs bedroom filled with all kinds of toys.

He was playing with them within minutes and continued to do so until his Mom called from downstairs, "Get down here right now and have some breakfast. Grandma fixed you those blueberry pancakes you like so much."

Actually, it was the third time his mom had called for him to come eat.

As Bobby watched Remington play, he looked around the tree branches and saw only a couple of his cousins down at the bottom of the tree who appeared to be awake. All the other lights were resting. They were exhausted.

Bobby was tired, but not as much as every other

bulb. He just seemed to have more energy.

And so, as he lie there wide awake, he thought how great the past two days had been.

The lights had been ablaze all Christmas Eve until at least 11 o'clock.

In fact, it was closer to Midnight when Remington had fallen asleep and Mr. "Mac" had CLOMPED back up the stairs to unplug the lights.

Then on Christmas morning the lights were on again by 7 o'clock, when Remington came hopping out of bed full of energy and ready to become even bigger friends.

"Good morning, Christmas tree, and Merry Christmas, you beautiful lights. Why don't you wake up and be happy like me?" Then Remington did what his mom and grandparents had told him not to do when he had finally been forced to go to bed the night before.

"Do not try and plug in the lights. It's hard to reach behind the cabinet."

Remington's mom had made sure he understood. "We'll turn them on first thing tomorrow morning just like grandma always does with the big tree downstairs. You know your grandma and grandpa. They turn the tree lights on ALL day on Christmas."

"But, mom, can't I turn them on if I get up earli-er?"

"No. Just call someone. One of us will come plug them in."

"But what if I get up real, real early and I don't want to wake you up?"

"Remington! That's enough," his mom had scolded. "Don't worry. You won't want to take time for that when you realize Santa's gifts are downstairs."

But she had been wrong.

When Mrs. McGillicuddy had finished making the downstairs tree bright at 8 o'clock, she headed up to "surprise" Remington when he woke up. But the "sur-prise" was on Mrs. McGillicuddy.

Remington was already playing with the presents that he had opened the night before, and sitting in the middle of the room staring at his tree which was ablaze with color.

"Those lights really do look brighter than any I've ever seen," Mrs. McGillicuddy muttered to herself be-fore looking at Remington. She wanted to fuss at him but just couldn't.

"I thought your mom told you not to turn those lights on by yourself because they are too difficult to plug in."

"I know, grandma, but I just had to. This is my tree and I love it and all the bulbs. They smiled at me last night when I fell asleep."

Mrs. McGillicuddy started to tell Remington he was being silly but decided not to. "How many times are you seven?" she had thought to herself.

"Alright. We'll keep this our secret. How long have you had them on?"

"Since 7 o'clock," Remington said proudly.

"Boy, you are the early riser."

"Yep!"

"Well, Mr. Early Riser, maybe you forgot about Santa Claus downstairs. I think I saw some presents and a couple of other toys that weren't there when we went to bed, and are you ever going to be surprised."

"Okay," said Remington. But it was one of those long drawn out "Okays" that means "okay", but not neces- sarily "okay".

"Okay what, little boy? Does that mean you are ready to come downstairs?"

"How 'bout ten minutes, grandma? Then I'll come."

By the time Remington made it downstairs the ten minutes had turned into an hour.

When Remington's father, who was the last person to wake up, finally yelled, "Get downstairs or Santa may come get these presents," Remington had slowly left the room, waving good-bye to his tree and the bulbs.

Moments later he had shrieked and screamed with joy when he discovered all the things Santa Claus had brought him, including a new bicycle that had no training wheels on it.

And thus Christmas Day became the exciting wonderful time it was supposed to be. It was a short visit and the McGillicuddys spent all day enjoying their gifts, the food, and the laughs and good times.

Bobby had felt a little sad as he heard Remington and his dad go out the front door to test the new bike. *"What is it about that kid?"* Bobby had said to himself, *"he's like part of our family."*

As the rest of the bulbs began to wake up, some had asked Bobby, *"Where's Remington?"*

"Is the little guy downstairs?"

And even one silly question from cousin Blushing, *"How can I be shining? I was sleeping."*

Christmas morning eventually turned into Christmas afternoon featuring a dining room table filled with turkey, dressing, cranberry sauce, mashed potatoes, green beans, beets, fluffy baked rolls, stuffed deviled eggs and of course, Mrs. McGillicuddy's famous corn casserole.

Intermingled with the passing of plates, the stories of past Christmas days, the pleas from Remington's mom and dad for his grandma to make more corn casserole next year, and Mrs. McGillicuddy's constant reminder that there was plenty of food left and everyone needed to eat more, came the laughter of a happy family on Christmas day.

From downstairs the conversation flowed freely up the stairwell and into the guest room where Bobby was able to understand much of the conversation, and enjoy the laughter. He knew this was his family's greatest Christmas ever.

17

Late Christmas Night

Remington was asleep in his bed.
The tree lights were dark.

It had been a marvelous day for Remington, and for Bobby Bright and his family.

Great fun, great food, lots of laughter and the enjoyment of the McGillicuddy family being together.

And for Bobby Bright a valuable lesson learned in the final hours of this very special Christmas.

Remington had stayed up until 10 o'clock and would have still been awake had his mom not finally demanded he turn out the lights and get into bed.

When he finally crawled into the four poster bed, he had stepped gingerly among all the gifts scattered on the floor and climbed up the two-step mahogany wood stool.

He had pleaded with his mom, "Keep the tree lights

on, mom. Don't turn them off, please!"

She had promised him they would remain lit until he was sound asleep.

But that didn't happen for another 30 minutes.

As soon as his mom had left the room, Remington sat straight up in the bed. When he heard her reach the bottom of the stairs and walk away to the back of the house, he had crawled from beneath the covers and sat at the end of the bed and stared at his Christmas tree and the bright strand of lights.

He had counted the bulbs. Twenty-five of them. They were all pretty but the blue one at the front of the tree was something special. Remington just knew it kept winking at him, even though it wasn't one of those "blinking" type lights.

"Hi, buddy," Remington had said.

Bobby recalled his mom nudging him and whispering, *"Don't you dare say a word, Bobby Bright."*

And Bobby had remained quiet, even though it was soooo tough to do.

Remington chattered to the tree and the lights in quiet whispers until finally he rolled over at the foot of the bed and just fell asleep.

"Hey, buddy. Wake up," Bobby shouted, and be-

fore his mom and dad could scold him for having spoken, Remington stirred, stretched his arms, put his face squarely upon the extra folded blanket which lay at the foot of the bed, and then bolted straight up.

"Is somebody here?" Remington asked.

He looked around the room, and then without another word, crawled back to the head of the bed, slipped under the sheet and two blankets, and pulled all of them tightly together up underneath his chin.

Bobby smiled to himself as Remington's head disappeared from view.

But then, almost immediately, up popped a flock of strawberry blonde hair and a freckled covered face.

"Good night, Christmas tree and you beautiful lights."

Bobby's parents said nothing for five minutes until they were sure Remington was asleep. And then Bobby Bright learned a valuable Christmas night lesson.

Even the most intelligent, wisest, neatest, smartest, funniest, and most magical Christmas tree light bulb in the entire world, still has to obey his parents.

They chewed him out in whispered tones for ten minutes as Bobby's brother, sister, cousins, uncles and aunts on the strand listened in amazement without saying a word. Bobby Bright was their leader, but even he still had to mind his mom and dad.

"I promise I won't do it again," Bobby said quickly to his father and then Mr. McGillicuddy CLOMPED up the stairs, entered the room and pulled the plug from the socket.

"*Wow!*" Bobby thought to himself, "*What a day. Every Christmas should be like this.*"

18
Bobby and Remington Get Closer

The next two days were the most wonderful ever. Remington hardly ever left the room.

"Remington. Come downstairs and see Grandma and Grandpa. You've been up there all morning."

It was the second day after Christmas.

"In a minute, mom, I just want to stay and look at my tree."

Remington stood in front of the tree looking like he might cry. "I don't want to go home tomorrow. I want to stay here," he said, as he looked at the tree and directly at Bobby Bright.

"This is too much, dad," Bobby whispered. *"We need to make sure that little guy never forgets us."*

"What are you going to do?"

As Remington stepped out of the room and yelled downstairs to his mom, Bobby shouted to all the bulbs,

"Make yourselves blink."

And that's exactly what happened because all of the bulbs except two had now discovered they too had extra magical powers.

"I'm coming, mom," Remington shouted, and then he turned and walked back into the room.

What a sight awaited him. Every bulb was the brightest it had ever been, and blinking on and off, on and off, as rapidly as possible. Remington's mouth flew open. His eyes opened so wide they actually hurt for a moment.

He turned and screamed downstairs, "Wow! Mom, Dad, come quick."

Then he looked back into the room and the air rushed from his lungs. As pretty as it had been seconds ago, it was even brighter and more colorful now.

Remington was standing like a statue when his mom came charging into the room. She took one look, turned and went back into the hallway and screamed for help.

"Hurry up! Something is wrong with Remington."

Then she stepped back in the room and grabbed Remington. She shook him hard. "Honey, what is it? Say something. Can you breathe?"

Then Remington moved and a huge smile broke out on his face.

"Does this mean you are okay?"

Before he could answer, his mom scolded him. "What is wrong with you? Are you trying to scare me?"

At that instant Rocket came tearing into the room barking wildly with Remington's dad only a few steps behind and out of breath and huffing and puffing. Finally Mr. and Mrs. McGillicuddy made it into the room.

"Get that dog out of the room," Remington's dad yelled.

"Oh my heavens! You look like you've seen a ghost, Remington," Mrs. McGillicuddy said, as she continued to try and catch her breath.

"*She's the one who looks like she's seen a ghost,*" Bobby leaned over and told his mom. "*She's whiter than cousin Whitening.*"

"Say something. Talk to me". Remington's dad sounded angry. "Are you joking with us?" he pleaded.

The smile quickly left Remington's face and his dad

grabbed him and shook him hard. "Are you alright, lit-tle guy?"

Remington appeared scared. "Are you mad at me, daddy?" He stared up at his father who reached down and hugged him.

"No, but your momma sounded scared. What hap-pened, Lisa?"

"He was standing there like he was in shock and couldn't breathe."

Mr. McGillicuddy had been quiet too long. "Tell grandpa what happened."

Remington looked first at his dad, then his mom, and then at the tree.

Bobby was sure he was looking straight at him and he was tempted to do what he had done less than a min-ute earlier. But he didn't. He just nestled against the branch and watched.

"See what you've done? They may throw us out forever."

"Don't worry, pops. They won't believe him," Bobby said as he listened to Remington try to explain.

"......and mom, the lights started blinking and then that one right there, mom," Bobby felt the thumb of Remington push him deep into the tree before letting go. "That one right there, mom, winked at me. I mean it, mom. It winked at me."

Mr. McGillicuddy started to chuckle. "Oh my little guy, you do know how to tell a story," and he patted Remington on his head.

"Don't make fun of me, grandpa. That bulb right there," and Bobby saw Remington point at him again, "... that one in the middle of the tree, the really dark, dark blue one, it winked at me."

Mrs. McGillicuddy waved her hand at Mr. McGillicuddy and put her finger to her lips and said quietly, "Shoosh," as he started to interrupt.

Then she reached down and hugged Remington and looked him straight in the eyes. "So you think those bulbs blinked at you again? This is getting to be a regular story."

Remington shook his head and pointed to the dark blue bulb in the middle of the tree. "No, grandma. They all blinked, but only that one winked at me." Remington pointed to the dark blue bulb in the middle of the tree.

"But don't you know these are non-blinking bulbs? Only one strand on the tree downstairs blinks."

"And those don't very often," Remington's dad butted in, "because grandpa keeps forgetting to put the blinker switch on."

Remington pulled away from Mrs. McGillicuddy and brushed against the front branches. "Sorry, my friends," he said and turned and looked at the lights. "They don't believe me. So please blink."

"They aren't going to blink, and they sure aren't going to wink," Mr. McGillicuddy laughed after making the bad rhyme.

And when he said that, Remington pulled away from his grandma and screamed, "No one ever believes me about anything."

Then he tore out of the room and went scooting down the stairs.

At the bottom he looked back up the stairs and shouted. "Go ahead and laugh. They won't blink for you because they are my friends and my bulbs and my tree."

"John McGillicuddy, you are something else. Isn't it interesting that two weeks before Christmas when you were drinking eggnog faster than you were putting the lights on the tree, you said the lights had winked at you."

And when Mrs. McGillicuddy said that, Remington's mom and dad broke into laughter.

"What's happening? Why are they laughing, Bobby?"
It was his brother who asked the question.
"I'll tell you later, Dimmer," he said.

19
December 28th

The car was packed full of luggage and Remington's gifts plus a few for his mom and dad.

"It's been great, mom," Remington's dad hugged Mrs. McGillicuddy. They walked into the guest room where Remington had stayed and checked under the bed to make sure there were no new toys left behind.

Mrs. McGillicuddy opened the closet door. "Nothing in here is his. Looks like you have everything."

"Thanks, mom. This was great having Remington sleep up here. The tree was a super idea. You know you will have to do it next year too."

"I know. That will be the fun part."

"Did you buy an extra strand of lights? These seemed newer than the ones downstairs. They sure did shine brighter."

"No, that's the weird part of all of this," said Mrs.

McGillicuddy. "In fact, Richard, this strand was headed to the junk pile. It looked like they were all burned out, but I was arguing with your dad about some silly thing and picked them up, brought them up here, and decided to put them on the tree. And lo and behold! Bingo! They worked like they were brand new."

"Well whatever, make sure you do the same thing next year."

"Oh, I will dear," and with that they walked out and down the stairs.

"What did they say?" Bobby's dad asked.

"Anything important?" Uncle Flicker yelled from the bottom of the tree.

"Listen up, everybody! I have good news," and then Bobby paused in dramatic fashion.

"Well, what is it?" came the squeaky voice of Aunt Shining.

"Duh Duh, drum roll please."

"What's wrong with him?" Bobby's mom scolded at no one in particular.

"Tell us and quit goofing around."

"Okay, Dad. Listen up, everyone."

"What do you think we are doing?" the voice of Uncle Flicker again from the bottom of the tree.

116

"Remington's dad thought we were as bright as brand new bulbs. He told Mrs. McGillicuddy to make sure next year she puts a tree up here with lights on it. And Mrs. McGillicuddy said she would."

The cheers rang out from every bulb, and every branch of the tiny tree shook.

Remington, his mom and dad, and Mr. and Mrs. McGillicuddy were all in the foyer hugging and chattering when Mr. "Mac" yelled. " What's that noise?"

Everyone quit talking, and sure enough it sounded like the television was on in the guest room upstairs.

"Did you leave the television on, love bug?"

But before Remington could answer his mom, Mrs. McGillicuddy said, "No, Lisa. Richard and I were just up there. We checked everything and the TV wasn't on."

"Time to go, guys," Remington's dad said. "Let's get in the car."

"Just a minute, daddy. I think I know what it is," and before anyone could tell Remington not to run upstairs, he did just that very thing.

He raced into the room.

117

"Remington. Come on, sweetie. We've got to go. Get back down here," his mom called from below.

"Oh my Gosh!" came the scream from upstairs. "You won't believe it."

"What is it now?" Mrs. McGillicuddy yelled.

Remington was standing on the landing at the top of the stairs. "Come quick, everyone."

And with that the four adults raced up the stairs yet one more time.

"*See what you've done?*" Bobby's dad twisted in his pod and tried to bump Bobby. But only Bobby had the power to do that.

"*Oh, dad. It's no big deal. I just winked and said be good buddy.*"

Then they heard the CLOMPING on the stairs.

"*Don't you move, Bobby Bright,*" his dad ordered, "*not one mega inch.*"

"It winked at me. And it talked to me, Mom. I swear. It happened."

Remington pulled his mother into the room. Right behind them came everyone else trying to catch their breath. When they heard Remington say, "It winked at me," they all began to laugh as they had done yesterday.

"I swear the bulb winked at me. And quit laughing." Then just like he had done yesterday, Remington started to whine and his lips puckered up as if he was going to cry, but this time instead of crying he shouted, "It happened. That bulb right there," and Remington jammed his index finger into the bluest bulb of all sitting directly in the middle of the tree.

"*Ouch!*" Bobby whispered.

"*Be quiet,*" his dad pleaded.

But it was way too noisy for anyone to hear them.

"So the bulb talked to you?" Remington's dad laughed.

"Yesterday, the bulbs were blinking out of control and winking at you and now they are talking. These really are different bulbs."

Now Remington couldn't hold it. He began to cry and sobbed, "No one believes me."

"Oh come on, buddy," Mr. McGillicuddy said. "Your grandpa believes you. I think I saw them wink at me when they were lying on the floor downstairs even before they were put on the tree."

119

"Yeah, dad," Remington's father said to Mr. Mc-Gillicuddy, "but Remington hasn't had any eggnog this morning."

And with that they all laughed some more.

But Remington didn't know what to do. He couldn't decide whether to keep crying or start laughing.

"Come on, Remington. If you say you saw a bulb wink, so be it. But don't tell me it talked to you."

And everyone laughed again and then Mr. McGillicuddy picked up his grandson, wiped the tears away, and they headed downstairs.

20

Good-bye Remington

When Remington and his mom and the McGillicud-dy's had left the room and gone downstairs, Remington's dad made an excuse he needed to wash his hands. He went into the bathroom which was around the corner from the bedroom.

He waited until everyone walked out the front door and onto the driveway. He then stuck his head back inside the bedroom and stared at the tree. He stood there for a moment before he walked over and touched the dark blue bulb nestled squarely in the middle. He took it between his index finger and forefinger and shook it a little.

"Nope, I don't hear anything. Guess you can't talk."

Then he chuckled to himself, turned and walked out of the room and down the stairs. Remington's mom stuck her head back inside the front door and yelled,

"Come on, honey."

Bobby said nothing until he heard Remington's dad open the door and go outside. Then he broke into laughter. And in "bulbese" he told everyone what had been said.

"He was checking to see if I could talk. How about that? Now remember, he was telling Remington how silly it was to say a bulb could talk, but he still was looking at me like he hoped I would."

The bulbs joined Bobby in more laughter.

"And," Bobby added, *"it hurt when he pinched my nose."*

And the bulbs laughed some more.

"Grandma. Tell Bobby I will see him next Christmas."

"Who's Bobby, sweetheart?" Mrs. McGillicuddy leaned down to the window of the car and gave Remington another kiss.

"Grandma. Don't play dumb with me. I'm seven now. You know who Bobby is. He's sitting right there in the middle of my Christmas tree with all the other lights."

"Tell grandma and granddaddy good-bye," Remington's mom said.

"Give them one more kiss."

And Remington did, sticking his head out of the back window and hugging both of his grandparents.

Then, surrounded in the back seat by all of the presents he had gotten for Christmas, he waved one more time as the car drove away.

When the car pulled around the corner, Mr. and Mrs. McGillicuddy quit waving and started to walk across the driveway and into the house.

But they had taken only a few steps when they heard the car horn honk. They turned and saw the car pass the grilled fence at the side of the house.

The back window was rolled down and Remington waved and shouted, "You know, Grandma, the dark blue one in the middle who talks."

End of Part Two

<u>Epilogue</u>

It was quiet downstairs. The clock in the foyer had just struck 12 noon.

The McGillicuddys had broken all tradition. They always took the Christmas tree down December 26th. But this year had been different because for the first time Remington and his mom and dad had been able to stay two extra days.

They had left both trees up so Remington could enjoy them.

Bobby could hear the McGillicuddys talking in the far distance. It was impossible to understand anything they were saying. But he knew they had been taking down ornaments and strands of lights since around nine o'clock when Remington and his parents had left.

Soon it would be time for Bobby and his family to join all those other strands that were being placed in the big box downstairs, and head to the dungeon. Another 11 months in the closet with a couple of days out for spring cleaning.

It was a sad time, but nothing like the previous years

when Bobby and his family had been unhappy almost all of the time. This year had truly been a miracle and Bobby knew his magical powers had made it possible.

It felt good and he took time to tell all of the bulbs how happy and fortunate they should be to have been able to make a little 7-year old boy, and for that matter, the whole McGillicuddy family happy.

They reminisced about the great times, about all the things they had laughed about, and the fact they had managed to shine so brightly the room had been a beautiful bouquet of Christmas colors.

Of course someone brought up Bobby's mischievousness in actually speaking to Remington, and everyone heehawed over that funny event too. Even Bobby's dad laughed, although he quickly told Bobby never to do anything like that again.

So there was lots of talking and laughing until shortly after noon when Mr. McGillicuddy came CLOMP, CLOMP, CLOMP up the stairs.

The next 30 minutes were not fun. Worn out from working all morning, Mr. "Mac" was in a hurry to get everything done. He quickly pulled the plug from the wall socket, then just as quickly drug the strand through the branches, and just simply wadded the cord into a big ball and tossed it on the bed.

A series of *"ouches"* poured from the mouths of most of the bulbs.

Of course Mr. McGillicuddy didn't hear them. He was humming "Rudolph the Red-Nosed Reindeer," intermingled with a few more slurps from his big mug that was filled with the last of the Christmas eggnog.

After each quick sip, he would grab some more ornaments and remove them from the tree.

It didn't take long and when he was finished, he pulled the little tree out of the tiny stand which sat atop the table. In a matter of moments he was out the door and the tree was headed for the end of the driveway with the other trash.

Fifteen minutes later Mr. McGillicuddy was back upstairs and he was definitely in a hurry. He tossed the ornaments into a bag instead of the box with the perfectly proportioned holes for each one. And then he scooped up the strand of lights with his left hand and placed them in the crook of his right arm and off down the stairs he CLOMPED.

Once in the foyer it was only a few steps to the huge box where he dropped the strand of lights on top of it, and then he continued on with the ornaments.

"*What's happening, Bobby?*" The questions came from everywhere.

"*I can see inside the box, Bobby.*" It was Uncle Flicker, who just had a knack of being in the most exciting places all of the time, whether on the tree or off of it.

"*What do you see, Uncle Flicker?*" Bobby shouted.

"*All the other bulbs are in the box.*"

"*What does that mean, Bobby?*" It was another voice from somewhere within the crumpled strand.

Now every bulb had a question, but Bobby ignored all of them.

He was thinking about what Uncle Flicker had said. Bobby could see his uncle and aunt clearly at the very end of the twisted cord, nearly hanging inside the hole that was formed by the four top sections of the box.

"*Is every strand inside the box, Uncle Flicker?*"

Bobby waited for a reply. And then he waited some more.

"*Hurry up. Are all the strands in the box?*"

This time Uncle Flicker answered. "*Yes, it looks like

it. But there may not be much room for us. It is hard to see."

There was a pause, and then, *"Yeah, as far as I can tell they are all there. But it's hard to be sure because there is a large white towel covering part of them."*

It took three or four seconds for what his Uncle had said to sink in and when it did Bobby couldn't resist a loud, *"Yahooooo!"*

"Now what?" It was Bobby's mom who had the next question.

"Good news, mom. Good news, everybody. We are on top and separated from the other nine strands underneath. That means we are being saved to go upstairs again next year."

And just as the bulbs started to send up a loud cheer, Bobby interrupted. *"Quiet. Here comes Mr. "Mac.""*

And then the good news turned bad.

Bobby would have all winter, spring, summer, and early fall to think about it. But most of all there would be all that time to worry about it.

Mr. McGillicuddy sat down the huge mug of eggnog as Mrs. McGillicuddy walked through the foyer headed to the master bedroom.

"John McGillicuddy, are you back drinking that eggnog again?"

"It's the last of it, dear."

"Well there seems to be a lot of that last part, John."

"I'm fine, dear," he said, and he reached down, picked up the huge box, took three steps forward, balanced on one foot, pulled the door back with his other leg and then suddenly tripped and fell forward as the box flew out of his hands spilling strands of bulbs across the floor.

Mrs. McGillicuddy had left the foyer while her husband was picking up the box. She was headed down the hallway toward the bedroom when she heard him fall, followed by the noise of Christmas lights bouncing everywhere.

She came running back. "Oh my gosh!" she screamed. "Look what you have done! Oh John, you are the biggest clutz ever."

Mr. "Mac" did not move.

"Get up, John," she demanded.

Mr. McGillicuddy didn't even stir slightly. In fact, he just laid there covered with lights and stretched across the smashed box. The strands were wrapped around his head and arms.

Had it not been such a mess, it would have been

downright funny.

But for Bobby Bright, buried in a tangle of bulbs and staring at his family intertwined with other strands outside the box, this was not funny.

Bobby knew one thing immediately. It would be impossible to recognize one strand of lights from another and that was going to mean trouble.

If Mr. and Mrs. McGillicuddy ever got all this mess untangled, the Bright family could wind up anyplace in the huge storage box.

And so it was. Just like that! One lousy stumble by old eggnog drinking Mr. McGillicuddy had changed everything.

There was no doubt. This had been "Bobby Bright's Greatest Christmas Ever", but would there ever be another one?

What will happen to Bobby and his family?

Will they ever be back on the little tree again?
Find out the amazing story that takes place and
the heartbreak that Bobby and his mom have.

Next Christmas be looking for:
  "BOBBY BRIGHT'S CHRISTMAS HEROICS"

Also Coming in future Christmas seasons:

"Bobby Bright Spends Christmas in Spain"

"Bobby Bright's Christmas as a Professor"

"Bobby Bright Meets His Maker"